T2-CBO-700

Under the SABBATH LAMP

For my mom, Charlotte Herman, who lit the way. –M.H.

To every child who loves books –A.M.

KAR-BEN PUBLISHING, INC.
A division of Lerner Publishing Group, Inc.
241 First Avenue North
Minneapolis, MN 55401 USA
1-800-4-KARBEN

Website address: www.karben.com

Library of Congress Cataloging-in-Publication Data

Names: Herman, Michael, 1964– author. | Massari, Alida, illustrator.
Title: Under the Sabbath lamp / by Michael Herman ; illustrated by Alida Massari.
Description: Minneapolis : Kar-Ben Publishing, [2017] | Age 3–8, K to Grade 3. | Summary: "Izzy and Olivia Bloom tell their Shabbat guests the story of their Sabbath lamp, which Izzy's great-great-great grandfather and his family brought piece-by-piece when the immigrated to America"—Provided by publisher.
Identifiers: LCCN 2016009543 (print) | LCCN 2016029189 (ebook) | ISBN 9781512408416 (lb : alk. paper) | ISBN 9781512408430 (pb : alk. paper) | ISBN 9781512427264 (eb pdf)
Subjects: | CYAC: Sabbath—Fiction. | Jews—Fiction. | Immigrants—Fiction.
Classification: LCC PZ7.1.H494 Und 2017+ (print) | LCC PZ7.1.H494 (ebook) | DDC [Fic]—dc23

LC record available at https://lccn.loc.gov/2016009543

Manufactured in the United States of America
1-39400-21214-6/8/2016

Under the
SABBATH LAMP

Michael Herman

Illustrated by
Alida Massari

KAR-BEN
PUBLISHING

From the day Izzy and Olivia Bloom moved into the neighborhood, they became everybody's favorite Shabbat dinner guests.

Every Friday evening, they were invited to a different family's home—to the Silvermans or the Applebaums, to the Kaplans or the Coopers.

They always arrived just before sundown.
Olivia with her tangy tart lemon bars, and Izzy
carrying a bottle of homemade cherry cordial.

The evenings began with the lighting of the Shabbat candles. Two tall white candles stood side by side in silver candlesticks. A special blessing was said, welcoming Shabbat. Then, as the candles flickered, everyone ate the festive meal and sang Shabbat songs.

There was lively conversation, and Izzy told his colorful stories:

"After the rainstorm, a family of ducks followed Olivia and me home from the synagogue. Then the whole family took a bath in a big puddle in our backyard!"

They ended each evening with Olivia's tangy tart lemon bars, and toasting *l'chayim* with Izzy's cherry cordial.

"To good health and to good friends—and to good times together!"

Week after week, Izzy and Olivia shared their neighbors' tasty Shabbat meals and warm friendship.

Then one week, Izzy and Olivia decided it was time for them to invite their new friends for Shabbat dinner.

On Friday they cooked, cleaned, baked lemon bars, and mixed a new batch of cherry cordial. Just before sundown, their guests arrived.

Everyone gathered in the dining room. The table was set with a lacy cloth and fancy dishes. A bottle of wine stood on the table along with a silver wine cup. Two braided challah loaves sat on a large platter.

But something was missing. Little Sadie Silverman noticed it first.

"Where are your Shabbat candles?" she blurted out

Izzy and Olivia exchanged smiles. "We don't light Shabbat candles," Olivia answered.

There were gasps all around.

Then Izzy and Olivia raised their heads and gazed up at the ceiling. So did everybody else.

Staring back at them was a shiny brass chandelier. It was shaped like a star, and it had no lightbulbs.

"Our Sabbath lamp," Izzy announced.

He reached up and grasped the long ratchet that held the lamp. Everyone watched as he lowered it, *click-click-click*.

Olivia carefully filled the star with olive oil, placed a wick into each point, lit the wicks, and said the blessing. The whole dining room filled with light.

Then under the Sabbath lamp, as they ate their festive meal, Izzy told them its story.

My great-great-grandfather, Isaac, lived in a small village in Germany where he raised chickens and cows.

Every Monday he said good-bye to his wife, Rachel, their son, Yussel, and their two daughters, Ruthie and Sophie. He traveled from town to town, selling his livestock, and returned home every Friday before the Sabbath.

On one of his trips, Isaac made a trade with a peddler—Isaac's plump chickens for a shiny brass Sabbath lamp.

Rachel, Yussel, Ruthie, and Sophie helped him hang it over their table. When they lit the lamp that night for the first time, the room was bathed in light, and their Sabbath meal became a grand feast.

It was hard for Isaac to make a living selling chickens and cows. It could be dangerous, too.

On one of his trips, Isaac's wagon got stuck in a ditch. You can imagine how happy he was when two travelers passed by and offered to help. And help they did. They helped themselves to all of Isaac's chickens!

The bandits tied Isaac to a wagon wheel, and there he stayed
until a kind farmer came by and set him free.

So Isaac and Rachel decided to take their family to
America, where life would be safer.

Isaac would go first, to find work and a place to live.
Then he would send for the rest of the family.

As Isaac packed his belongings, Rachel handed him the drip pan from the Sabbath lamp.

"Take this with you," she told him. "Just as this part is separated from the rest of the lamp, we will be separated from you. When we come to join you, we will bring the other parts, and the lamp will be whole again. Just like our family."

In America, Isaac found work. And when he had saved enough money, he sent for Yussel, who arrived with the oil runners from the Sabbath lamp.

Over the months, the rest of the family arrived.
Ruthie brought the star,

Sophie brought the stem,

and Rachel brought the ratchet.

In their small apartment they hung the Sabbath lamp piece by piece. And on their first Sabbath together in this new land, they lit the lamp, which was whole again—just like their family.

When Izzy finished telling the story, he gazed up at the dancing flames.

"This lamp has been in our family for more than one hundred and fifty years," he said. "When Olivia and I were married, my parents entrusted it to us."

"What a beautiful story," said Lila Silverman. "It reminds me of a Shabbat tablecloth that has been in my family for many years. It's covered with old wine and gravy stains that never quite washed out. And for every stain there is a story of how it got there. We love that tablecloth. Stains and all."

Eli Kaplan nodded. "You inherited a tablecloth. I inherited a melody. It was composed by my grandfather, who was a musician."

Then Eli started singing. Before long, everyone around the table caught the melody and sang with him.

"We've all inherited treasures," said Izzy.

"I know what I want to inherit," said little Sadie Silverman. "Lemon bars!"

As everyone laughed, Olivia passed around her tangy tart lemon bars. And with his homemade cherry cordial, Izzy toasted *l'chaim* to their family of friends, all sitting together, under the Sabbath lamp.

A Note about the Hanging Sabbath Lamp

Every Friday before sundown, Jewish families welcome
Shabbat by kindling the Shabbat lights. Today most
people light candles held in candlesticks. But long ago,
special oil lamps were used (PICTURED, RIGHT). They hung
from the ceiling, often above the dining table. These
lamps not only ushered in Shabbat but provided light
for the Shabbat meal.

About the Author and Illustrator

MICHAEL HERMAN has a passion for Jewish history and tradition, and enjoys
collecting antique Judaica. Every Friday evening he lights a 19th century
hanging Sabbath lamp of his own. Michael lives in Chicago, Illinois. This is
his first children's book.

ALIDA MASSARI is an Italian artist specializing in illustration for children.
Born in Rome where she completed a specialization in illustration at the
European Institute of Design, she finds inspiration for her work from folk
traditions and ancient art. She has illustrated many books, collaborating with
Italian, English, German and American publishers. She lives in Rome, Italy.